A Gift for Gracelyn

A Gift for Gracelyn

A. E. SMITH

RESOURCE *Publications* • Eugene, Oregon

A GIFT FOR GRACELYN

Resource Publications
An Imprint of Wipf and Stock Publishers
199 W. 8th Ave., Suite 3
Eugene, OR 97401

www.wipfandstock.com

PAPERBACK ISBN: 978-1-5326-7176-0
HARDCOVER ISBN: 978-1-5326-7177-7
EBOOK ISBN: 978-1-5326-7178-4

Manufactured in the U.S.A.   JANUARY 10, 2019

For Kenna Marie

Other books by A. E. Smith

Journey of the Pearl

Contents

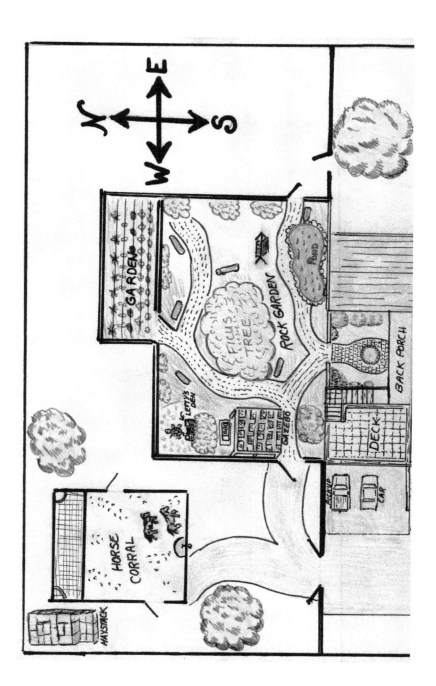

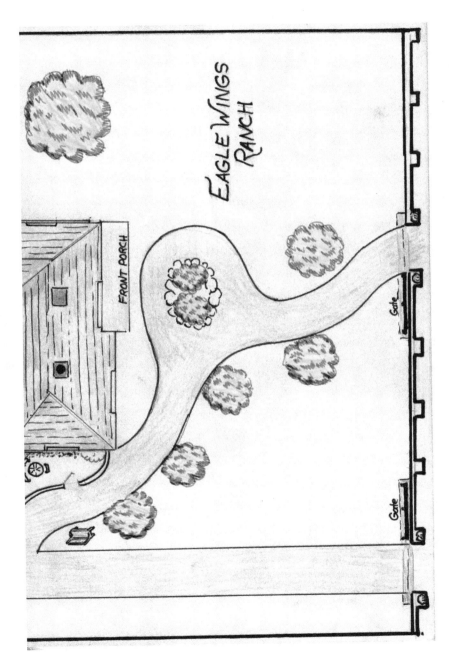

1

Lefty Learns Something

IT WAS LATE SPRING at the little ranch known as Eagle Wings in Arizona. Lefty, a desert tortoise poked his nose outside of his burrow and sniffed the air. Lefty enjoyed the delicate scent of the sage, verbena, and clover that grew wild on the Eagle Wings ranch. At the center of Eagle Wings sat a peach-colored house. Behind the house was a rock garden with desert trees and flowers enclosed by a block wall. Rabbits and prairie dogs enjoyed the protection of the garden walls from harsh dry winds, and the desert plants provided food for the animals. There was a pond in the garden that had fresh, clean water for the animals to drink. A gazebo shaded several picnic tables and the barbeque grill. Lefty would come out of his burrow to watch when the family that lived at Eagle Wings had a picnic. He liked to listen to them talk and to eat the lettuce they always offered him.

The garden walls were covered with orange jubilee shrubs which sprouted flowers called hummingbird trumpets. The hummingbirds enjoyed this delicious nectar so much they would save it for dessert. All of the birds at Eagle Wings loved the mesquite, sweet acacia, and eucalyptus trees, as well as a huge ficus tree that grew in the center of the rock garden. The ficus tree had long, strong branches with small leaves that blocked the gusts of desert winds. The birds knew that their nests would not blow away, and their babies would be safe. The rock garden was a good place for both animals and plants.

There was a block wall at the front of Eagle Wings which had two giant wrought-iron gates. There were pillars on either side of the gates. On top of each pillar sat a concrete sculpture of an eagle. Their wings were spread as if they could take flight at any moment. Yet, their talons forever grasped the tops of the pillars. Lefty thought the statues looked like real eagles when there was a full moon at night.

While Lefty was eating clover and verbena petals, he heard familiar voices.

"Let's sit out here," said Gracelyn, the eleven-year-old girl who lived at Eagle Wings with her fourteen-year-old brother, Terry, and their mom and dad. Included in the family were three dogs, Merlin, Jax, and Sunny; two cats, Pixel and Dot; two horses, Pepper and Dolly; and, of course, Lefty.

"Okay," said Terry as he ran his fingers through his red hair. "Do you want to set baseballs on the T-stand for me? I need to practice my swing. The last game for the school year is next week." He put his baseball cap on to shade his brown eyes from the sun's glare.

"Sure," said Gracelyn. Her hazel eyes brightened as she nodded happily. She pulled a rubber band from her pocket to put her long, dark hair into a ponytail. She liked to help her big brother practice for his games.

Gracelyn wasn't able to run and play as other children did because she was born with a damaged heart. She became tired very quickly and sometimes had trouble breathing. Terry felt sad for Gracelyn because he could do everything he enjoyed. He loved sports like baseball and track. He was especially good at hitting homeruns and running sprints and hurdles. Gracelyn's favorite thing to do was sing and she sang very beautifully. People said it made them happy to hear her sing. Terry wished she could sing as long and as loudly as she wanted, but she couldn't. She couldn't even sing a whole song without getting out of breath. Gracelyn never complained because Terry always found a way to include her in his activities. She loved to watch his baseball games and track meets, but she had to sit quietly without jumping up and down to cheer. The family hoped that Gracelyn's heart would be healed someday soon.

Gracelyn loved to be outdoors. The beauty and scent of the flowers, bushes, and desert trees made her happy. She carefully set a baseball on the T-stand and retreated to a bench under the giant ficus tree. Terry took a few practice swings before he stepped to the proper spot. He swung the bat and the ball flew into a net. Terry and Dad had made the net just for that purpose. Their mom and dad came out of the house and sat down with Gracelyn. Dad was carrying his sketchbook. He started drawing Gracelyn and Terry, his favorite subjects.

"We just got a call from your doctors, Gracie," Mom said. "Everything has been approved for your final operation. It's scheduled for May 30th at the hospital in the same town where Grandma and Grandpa live."

Lefty stopped chewing. He moved closer to listen.

"How long will Gracie have to stay at the hospital?" asked Terry.

Mom thought for a moment. "They said to expect a three-week stay."

"Gracie's birthday is June 8th," Terry exclaimed. "She will still be in the hospital. How are we going to have a birthday party?"

"Terry, it's okay," Gracelyn reassured him. "We can have a party when I get home. Then we can celebrate my birthday, *and* my happily-healed heart." She grinned at her brother. "It'll be the best party ever."

"If we're going to have to postpone your birthday party, then we should make it extra special," declared Terry. Mom and Dad agreed.

Lefty thought so, too. He knew how much Gracelyn loved birthdays and not just her birthday, but anyone's birthday. Gracelyn believed that birthday parties were a reward for having spent a year of doing nice things for others. Birthday parties were always a big deal with the family at Eagle Wings. Everyone was invited to enjoy the games and prizes, colored balloons, pretty decorations, music, and lots of good food. Lefty smiled to think of how much fun the parties were. The curious tortoise moved even closer.

"We'll work it out," said Dad. "The most important thing is for Gracelyn to have this operation." He looked at Gracelyn. "It will be the happiest day of our lives when you can run, and play, and sing to your heart's content."

"So it's all set up," said Mom. "Gracelyn, you'll have your own room in the hospital and it has a little patio. The wall facing the patio is all glass with a sliding glass door, so you'll be able to see the outdoors from your bed. I know you'll like that."

"Will I be able to stay there, too?" asked Terry. "School will be over."

"Yes, in fact we're counting on you, Terry," said Mom. "We can only miss work for a few days when Gracie has the operation. In fact, Grandma and Grandpa will come here and take you guys to the hospital a few days before the surgery. After that, your dad and I can come back only on the weekends. Gracie will need her big brother." Terry and Gracelyn exchanged a smile. They would be able to play chess, card games, and video games.

"Terry, will you read to me when I get tired?" asked Gracelyn.

He wrinkled his nose. "Can I read the Shivers & Shrieks stories?"

Gracelyn laughed. "Of course, you know I love scary stories. We can even make up our own stories."

Terry grinned. "It's a deal. I'll sketch the stories like a comic book and you can color in the pictures."

"Don't make your stories too scary," said Dad. "We don't want Gracelyn's heart to race to the moon—without her." Both children laughed at the idea of a flying heart.

"After the operation," said Terry, "Gracie will be able to sing all the way to the stars and back without missing a beat." Dad smiled and nodded agreement.

"Your sketch book will come in handy, Terry," said Mom. "You can draw whatever you two see outside the glass wall. There are flower beds along the patios, but nothing has been planted yet since this section of the hospital is brand new. Maybe there will be a tree nearby, and we can put up a birdfeeder so you can watch the birds."

"I'm going to miss everyone and everything here at Eagle Wings," said Gracelyn. "I hope our animal friends here won't worry about me and Terry while we're gone. I wish we could take them with us."

Terry loved the animals at Eagle Wings as much as Gracelyn did. He enjoyed drawing, especially animals and nature scenes. Gracelyn loved how the rabbits, prairie dogs, and birds would gather near when she was well enough to sing. Terry often sat with her and would sketch as many animals as he could. If they both sat very still, the animals would stay even when Gracelyn became too out of breath to sing.

When Terry went back to batting the baseballs from the T-stand, Gracelyn watched her father as he drew quick strokes on the paper. "Draw us happy, Daddy."

"That will be easy to do, Baby Girl. I love to draw your smiles best of all."

Lefty bobbed his head as he listened. He was beginning to form a plan for Gracelyn. A swish of color flew past the ficus tree. There was a throaty *pureeet* birdcall and Christopher, a flycatcher, landed on a branch of a mesquite tree. Christopher had gray feathers on his head and back and a yellow tummy. When flycatchers were excited, they could raise bushy feathers on the tops of their heads. The raised feathers looked like little party hats so it was perfectly natural that they fluffed up their feathers when they were happy.

Christopher folded his wings carefully and winked at Lefty. However, before he could get properly settled on the branch, a fly whizzed past. He flew off after it.

Dad fanned his face with his hand. "It really is getting hot out here. Look, there's Lefty, out of his burrow. I'll get him some romaine lettuce, his favorite." Dad laid his sketchbook down and went into the house. He returned with the lettuce and set it down under the shade of a sweet acacia tree. The bright yellow, ball-shaped puffs on the tree gave out a wonderful scent. Honey bees gathering pollen buzzed around the yellow puffballs. Lefty ambled up to the lettuce and began eating. The bees were intent on their work and paid no mind to Lefty.

As Lefty ate his lettuce, he heard a low buzzing and a high pitched *tweeeeeett*. The tortoise looked up and saw Mr. and Mrs. Hummingbird hovering overhead. He bobbed his head with a cheerful greeting. The hummingbirds answered Lefty with happy *chip-ip-ipper-ing* and settled on a low lying tree branch.

Terry gathered the baseballs into a bucket and sat down next to Gracelyn. "I sure hope this will be your last operation," he said. "I feel bad that you have been sick all your life."

"Don't feel bad, Terry. I know that when I'm well, I will enjoy it twice as much as people who were never sick like me. But even if this operation doesn't work, I'll still have you and Mom and Dad and all the animals here at Eagle Wings to make me feel better."

Lefty was very happy to hear that. Contented, he went back to munching his lettuce. The hummingbirds tilted their heads in agreement. They fluttered their tiny wings and looked down at Lefty with occasional *chiiiip*-s and *tweeeet*-s.

Gracelyn sighed. "I'm getting a little tired."

"Let's go in and cool off," said Mom. The family went inside.

Lefty finished his lettuce. He rested in the shade and thought about everything he had heard. He was concerned about Gracelyn being in the hospital on her birthday. However, Lefty was a smart tortoise and he had a wonderful idea, but he would need help.

Lefty looked around for the pair of hummingbirds. They were busily sipping nectar from the orange jubilee shrubs. "Hey, you two," Lefty called out. "Did you know that Gracelyn is having a birthday soon?"

"No, dear, we didn't," answered Mrs. Hummingbird. "How exciting! We should help her celebrate." Mr. Hummingbird wholeheartedly agreed.

Lefty was eager to share his idea. "My thought exactly, but we need help. Can you two spread the word to everyone at Eagle Wings? We need to have a meeting before the sun sets. Tell everyone to meet in our usual place by the corral."

Pepper and Dolly lived in the corral at Eagle Wings. Pepper was a dapple-gray mustang pony. Dolly was a black and white pinto pony. Dolly and Pepper were best friends even though they sometimes fussed at each other. Sometimes they didn't want to share when Gracelyn and Terry brought them carrots or apples. But they would share anyway because they were true friends.

The hummingbirds eagerly buzzed away to the corral. Soon, they were talking with Dolly and Pepper. Then the rabbits and prairie dogs came to listen. Henry and Lizzy, a pair of red-tailed hawks, saw them from the air and flew down to join them. In no time, the sparrows showed up, always eager to know the latest news. The call for a meeting would spread quickly throughout the ranch now that the sparrows were in on it.

Lefty thought about Gracelyn and Terry as he made his way out to the corral. He remembered how the kids took care of him when he was a baby tortoise. Lefty had his own plastic terrarium with a heat lamp to keep him warm, rocks to rest on, and a little wooden burrow to sleep in, and plenty of food and water. Sometimes Gracelyn would sing to him while Terry drew sketches of him. When the kids came home from school each day, they would take him out into the sun to make his shell strong. When Gracelyn was too sick to go to school, she would ask Mom to put Lefty's little terrarium next to her in bed so they could be together.

Whenever the children took Lefty outside, they never left him alone while he ate grass and clover. They would gently pick him up and take him back to his terrarium when he had been outside long enough. It wasn't long before he was big enough to live in the rock garden. The family helped Lefty build his burrow. Dad dug a hole in the ground and put a plastic dog house in the hole. Mom and the kids covered most of it with soil and planted grass and clover over the roof. Lefty smoothed out a dirt pathway down into the dog house. It was a wonderful burrow and it could never collapse. It was cool in the summer and cozy in the winter when Lefty hibernated. Gracelyn and Terry came out every day to visit him. Lefty always came out of his burrow when he heard their voices. The tortoise smiled to think that he and the children would always be friends.

2

A Call to Order

THE SUN BEGAN TO slip down toward the west. Lefty made his way to the corral. To his satisfaction, most of the animals had already gathered when he arrived. Pepper and Dolly were tossing their heads and trotting around the corral. Henry and Lizzy Hawk were watching their children play tic-tac-toe in the sand. The youngest prairie dogs were making necklaces with desert verbena stems. The littlest rabbits were playing hide-and-seek among the creosote bushes. The moms, dads, and grandparents were discussing the possible reasons for the meeting.

Lizzy Hawk looked up at the utility wires strung along the road in front of the ranch. The cactus wrens—white, black, and tan spotted birds—were landing on the wires. "I see the cactus wrens are gathering in their usual manner," she commented.

Now and again, another cactus wren would fly in and join their relatives and friends, making a rather long row of birds on the utility lines. From their vantage point, they could watch everyone below. The wrens discussed possible reasons for the meeting with their soft *chuh—chuh—chuh* sounds and much louder *Chug—Chug—Chug* calls. They sounded like a train when it slowly starts to move and then gains speed. The wrens also enjoyed watching the prairie dogs and rabbits hopping and popping around. It was amusing to see the moms and dads chasing after their spirited children. For every meeting that anyone could remember, the cactus wrens always showed up last. The other animals thought the wrens liked to make a grand entrance. Finally, the wrens flew down from the utility lines with much *chuh-chuh-chuh*-ing and wing fluttering. The cactus wren was the official state bird of Arizona and they were very proud of that title. Other birds occasionally asked a cactus wren for an autograph which he or she gladly scratched across a leaf.

Willie Rabbit was too busy to notice the cactus wrens. He was helping his wife, Rosemary, round up their many children who kept scampering in and out of clusters of fairy dusters and Indian paintbrushes. The fairy duster bushes had dark-pink, curly flowers surrounded by sprigs of soft bristles of the same color. The Indian paintbrush plants had pale-green stalks with feathery, red clusters of blossoms.

Tommy and Beatrice Prairie Dog were attempting to gather their family together. Their children had finished making verbena necklaces and were popping in and out of their ground tunnels. Tommy Prairie Dog stamped his feet and the children scurried obediently to their parents. Tommy counted the children. Someone was still missing. The youngest child, Little Sally Prairie Dog, was hiding behind a clump of golden desert snapdragons. She giggled as she waved a yellow and red-freckled snapdragon to get her dad's attention. Tommy rolled his eyes and sighed. Beatrice tried not to giggle and gave Little Sally a nip for teasing her daddy. Little Sally wiggled behind a rock to hide again.

She called to her daddy, "Can you see me now?"

She snickered until she saw his disapproving look. Little Sally decided she better behave, so she sat down with her parents. The rest of the prairie dog clan, including cousins, aunts, uncles, and grandparents, settled down as well.

Jacob and Katie Finch also lived at Eagle Wings. The finches had bright red feathers across the tops of their heads and matching red feathers down their fronts. They looked like they were wearing red beanies with red bibs. As soon as the family joined the assembly, the finch children greeted their friends, with excited *tiiicks* and *che-urr* finch-talk, but soon grew quiet. They were curious and eager to get started.

The finches found a place to sit next to their closest nest neighbors, a pair of roadrunners.

Nana and Pappy Roadrunner were favorites of all the children at Eagle Wings. Nana showed them how to make their own books from bits of colored paper and yarn that the wind carelessly tossed across the desert. Pappy was the track coach for the prairie dog and rabbit children. He believed that animals with legs should exercise them every day, just for fun. Of course, Pappy also had wings, which he fluttered with pride. When he volunteered to be the track coach, he mentioned that being "multi-mobile" would make him a good coach. The Eagle Wings committee was very impressed and hired him on the spot.

To add to the excitement, a whole clan of burrowing owls silently glided down from the sky. They carefully found their way around the other animals and seated themselves among a patch of Texas sage. The small brown birds blended in well with the lavender blossoms of the sage bushes. They were almost hidden from sight. Coming to a meeting was a most unusual thing for burrowing owls to do. They were shy birds who did not like to attract attention. Even their homes were hidden from view. The owls dug burrows in the ground like the prairie dogs. They rarely spoke even a single chirp when they attended a meeting. However, the excitement of the other animals caused a great deal of owl head-swiveling.

"My goodness gracious!" exclaimed Teresa Owl in her high mellow *coo-co-hoo coo-hoo*. "I've never seen so many animals turn out for a meeting!"

Teresa's brother, Jimmy, agreed. He scanned the group to see if all his friends were present. "Look, Sis," he *coo-co-hoo*-ed. "Even the doves are here. I don't think I've *ever* seen them at a meeting." The dove clan meant well, but tended to be a bit disorganized.

True to their usual restless behavior, the doves wandered among the clusters of animal clans. Their mournful *ooah, cooo, cooo, coo, ooah, cooo cooo, coo* dove-talk blended in with the rest of the noisy animal talk.

Then the sparrow clan swooped in, and the noise got even louder. No one was surprised to see the sparrows. They were curious birds, and they came to every meeting. Their piercing *cheeep cheeep cheeep* sparrow-talk blended in with the other birdsongs.

From his perch in a mesquite tree, Christopher Flycatcher saw that the meeting was about to start. He flew to his family's nest which was snugly hidden under the patio roof. Fiona Flycatcher, his wife, was reminding their twin boys, Larry and Jerry, how to act properly at a meeting. Even though the boys had gone to several meetings, Christopher and Fiona thought it a good idea to go over the rules each time.

Before Fiona could finish, Jerry chirped impatiently, "Yes, yes, Mommy, we know we're not to speak without permission." His flycatcher-talk was accented with the distinct *come-here come-here come-here* chirp that flycatchers used when they were the most excited.

"Jerry," warned his father gently with a soft *pwit pwit pwit*, "don't interrupt your mother."

"I'm sorry, Mom," he said with a soft *purreeet*. "I'll try to do my best."

Fiona smiled and patted his head with her wing. Larry winked at his brother. Jerry winked back with a smile. The family left their nest and flew to the horse corral. They couldn't wait to find out why Lefty had called a meeting.

The horses, being tall animals, could see that the gathering had gotten quite large. Pepper pawed the ground impatiently. "Come on, Lefty, the suspense is killin' me! Is anyone still missing?" she neighed.

Dolly tossed her head eagerly and snorted. "We're all about to pop from the suspense, Lefty! Can you give us a hint?"

Lefty was about to speak when he realized that the three dogs and two cats had not come out of the house yet. "Where's Sunny and Jax and Merlin?" he asked anxiously. "Where's Dot and Pixel? Did anyone tell them about the meeting?" Everyone looked around, but no one seemed to know.

"That's okay," piped up Pappy Roadrunner. "I'll go get 'em!" Off he raced toward the house and slipped in the doggie door. He soon returned. "I told Merlin and the cats but I couldn't find Sunny and Jax. I'll go look for them."

"Oy, bloke, 'ere we are," shouted Sunny with her British accent. Sunny was an English Jack Russell terrier and Jax was an English fox terrier. The two terriers had been sitting on hay bales the whole time.

"Blimey, Lefty, ol' chap! Didn't think we'd let the lot of you go straight away wi'out us, did ya?" asked Jax.

Sunny and Jax were cousins. They both came from England when they were just puppies. "It's been a jolly good show so far," added Sunny. They jumped down off the bales and trotted up to Lefty. Finding room among some Apache plum with gray, fuzzy leaves and pink, feathery flowers, they politely sat down. The British are very polite and Jax and Sunny were very British.

"We hope this will be a proper council," woofed Jax. A breeze whiffed playfully through a cluster of desert pincushions, tiny, pinkish-white, flowers that blossomed together in clumps. Several ladybugs were happily slurping nectar from the pincushions.

Sunny was a feisty little dog. She enjoyed chewing her toys and playing with Jax and Merlin. But it was Gracelyn who made her the happiest of all. Sunny waited by the front door every afternoon for her to come home from school. She jumped with joy when she heard the school bus turn around in front of Eagle Wings. Gracelyn would greet Sunny as soon as she came in the door. Every night, Sunny would curl up on the end of Gracelyn's bed. The little terrier always wanted to be near Gracelyn.

Jax was a little bigger than Sunny. He loved to retrieve tennis balls that Terry hit with his bat. Terry would praise Jax when he brought the balls back. Sometimes Jax would run before Terry hit the ball, leap in the air, and catch the tennis ball before it hit the ground. Terry would cheer for Jax when he jumped really high to catch a ball.

The meeting still couldn't start without Merlin and the cats. Lefty looked in the direction of the house, which was a good distance from the corral. Desert tortoises have surprisingly good vision so Lefty could easily see when Merlin came toward them from the rock garden.

Merlin was a big, powerful dog. His face, back, and legs were jet black. He had tall, black ears. His chest, tummy, and front paws were white with dark gray spots. But Merlin had something that was unusual for a dog. He had sky-blue eyes. His mother, a Siberian husky, also had blue eyes. She was a sled-dog for a rescue team in Alaska that saved people who were lost in snowstorms. Merlin's father was a German shepherd who was also on a rescue team. He was trained to save people trapped in buildings that had been damaged by earthquakes or storms. Merlin wanted to be like his parents so he dedicated his life to protecting Gracelyn, Terry, Mom, Dad, and his friends. Jax and Sunny helped Merlin keep watch over everyone who lived at Eagle Wings. Even the tiniest baby hummingbirds could depend on the trio of faithful dogs to make sure they stayed safe.

Just behind Merlin, the cats strolled out of the gate and gracefully stepped around families of rabbits and prairie dogs. Dot and Pixel were sister and brother. Dot was a charcoal-colored cat with a cream-colored undercoat that showed through when her fur was ruffled. Pixel had silvery-gray fur with dark markings. They kept their fur well-groomed and clean. Pixel and Dot prided themselves on always being perfectly presentable, as any respectable cat would.

Pixel and Dot spotted Jax and Sunny. The cats flicked their tails excitedly as they joined the little dogs. Merlin stopped to help a June bug get free from a tangle of desert dandelions. The little beetle had gotten stuck among the yellow petals. Merlin nudged the insect gently with his nose as he carefully separated the stems of dandelions.

"Thank you, Mr. Merlin," squeaked the June bug as he flew away.

"You're welcome, Mr. June Bug," answered Merlin.

Lefty waited for Merlin to join him. "Merlin, my furry friend, would you be so good as to bark this meeting to order?"

"It will be my honor." Merlin raised his head. "Bark! Bark! Bark!" he declared in his most commanding tone. "This meeting is hereby in session." A hush settled over the animals. They waited with great anticipation to hear what Lefty had to say.

3

The Meeting

LEFTY CLIMBED TO THE top of a mound of dirt while Merlin lay down near a clump of desert mariposa lilies. The bright orange lilies looked like delicate orange teacups. Several butterflies were sipping nectar from them as if they were having a tea party.

Lefty began to speak. "Okay everyone, listen up! I have called this meeting to discuss a very important idea." They pressed in, eager to hear. A friendly breeze swept past Lefty to help carry his words. He glanced at the horizon and saw that a dust storm was approaching. The gentle breeze would be pushed aside by a strong wind soon. Lefty continued, "Gracelyn is having a birthday soon and I think that we should . . ."

Sunny jumped in the air with joy. "Is Gracelyn having a party? That's brilliant! She always gives me a birthday party. Can we give her a party as well?"

Jax yipped in agreement. "We must give her a proper birthday party. We can play pin the tail on the tortoise and have races and . . ."

Lefty pushed up on his front legs and raised his voice. "Sunny! Jax! There is a problem! Gracelyn has to have an operation only a few days before her birthday. She will be away at the hospital for several weeks before she can come home. Terry, Mom and Dad are going to have a party for her when she gets home, but I think she needs a gift *on her birthday.*" He summarized the project with one sentence. "We have to decide what to give to her, and how we will get it to her on June 8th while she's at the hospital."

Little Sally leaned her head to one side. She raised a paw and asked, "Why does Gracelyn have to go to the hospital? Couldn't she have her operation here at Eagle Wings?" The animals muttered in agreement.

Jerry Flycatcher thought he had a solution. He elbowed his twin, and flittered up and down, flapping his wings, "I have an idea that would be even better! How 'bout *we* have the operation *for her,*" he suggested triumphantly. "Then she won't have to go to the hospital. She can have her party on her real birthday." He was fluttering his wings so excitedly, he lost his balance. Fortunately, Jerry flopped into a bunch of Mojave monkey flowers and landed in the flat-faced, white blossoms. He nearly disappeared among the reddish-purple leaves.

Merlin smiled at the little flycatcher child patiently. "That's a nice idea, Jerry, but operations don't work that way. Gracelyn must have the operation so she will feel better and it has to be done in the hospital. We need to think about a gift she will enjoy while she's in the hospital. Something very special."

Larry Flycatcher smiled around at them. "I bet if we give her the best gift ever, she'll get well quicker and come home sooner." He patted his heart with a wing tip for emphasis. Jerry nodded at Larry in happy agreement.

Lefty felt that the wind was getting a bit stronger so he raised his voice. "Please, everyone, may I continue?"

Pepper and Dolly tossed their heads at the dusty horizon. Henry and Lizzy Hawk pointed at the dirt-brown sky in the east. The animals knew they needed to hurry.

Lefty bobbed his head in his usual manner and continued. "So we need to come up with some ideas for a gift. It must be a single gift that comes from all of us here at Eagle Wings. Most importantly, it must be a gift that shows our love for Gracelyn because that's what gifts are for."

With that goal, the animals started talking excitedly! Mr. and Mrs. Hummingbird rose in the air and hovered above each family. Their *bzeee bzeee* squeaks and sharp little *chiiips* could be heard as they added in their own ideas. Tommy and Beatrice Prairie Dog huddled with their children to ask what kind of gifts they liked most.

Their high pitched squeaks proved they had lots of favorites. Willie and Rosemary Rabbit whispered with their children. They didn't want to be as loud as the prairie dogs. However, the rabbits indulged in much head nodding, ear flopping and nose wiggling. Christopher and Fiona Flycatcher were deep in thought while Jerry and Larry made loop-the-loops in the air. Dolly and Pepper raced around the corral, kicking up their heels and swishing their tails. The whole Finch family started chattering with lots of *wheeer* and *che-urrr* chirps, for emphasis. Lizzy and Henry Hawk flapped their wings and started talking to each other at the same time. Their children joined the lively discussion with *keeer-r-r keee-r-r keee-r-r*, the way Hawks talked when they were excited. Jax and Sunny discussed ideas in very precise British terms. Merlin gave Lefty a good-natured grin. This was going to take some time.

Lefty asked Merlin to call the meeting to order. The big Siberian stood up and barked, "Okay everybody, come to order." Merlin dipped his head at Lefty for him to continue.

"We need ideas for the gift," announced Lefty. "It must be something that will show how much we appreciate everything that Gracelyn does for us. Both Terry and Gracelyn have always been good to us. The two of them give me lettuce and keep me company while I eat. They put bits of cloth and yarn out for the sparrows, wrens, doves, flycatchers, finches, roadrunners and hawks when it's time to build nests." The birds nodded in agreement. "Terry makes sure the sugar water holder is full for the Hummingbird family. Gracelyn puts nuts and vegetables out for the Prairie Dog and Rabbit families during the autumn and winter."

Tommy Prairie Dog and Willie Rabbit hugged their wives and children, remembering how hungry they would have been without Gracelyn's and Terry's help.

"Terry brushes Pepper and Dolly," continued Lefty. "Gracelyn gives them carrots and apples. They also make sure Pepper and Dolly get enough exercise."

The horses swung their tails happily. "They do. They do. And Terry trims our manes while Gracelyn brushes our tails." They pranced around their corral. This stirred up a bit of dust but no one minded.

Pixel waved a paw. "Gracelyn helped Terry build our cat trees. We have one in Gracelyn's room and one in Terry's room. That way, Dot and I can take turns playing or sleeping in their rooms."

"Gracelyn feeds us right on time every day," said Dot, "and never forgets."

Merlin yipped in agreement. "Gracelyn makes sure the right amount of food is in each of our bowls—a little for Sunny, a bit more for Jax, and a lot more for me." He glanced at Sunny and Jax. "Of course, I'm about ten times bigger than Sunny."

Sunny pawed at an ear and sniffed. "I might be a little rascal, but I'm feisty."

Lefty looked around at his friends. "Let's have some ideas. Anyone?"

The animals quieted down. They were deep in thought. They thought and they thought. Finally, Little Sally popped a paw into the air. "I know. How 'bout we send Gracelyn a sunset? She loves sunsets!"

"And sun*rises*, too," added Rosemary Rabbit. "I've seen Terry draw the sunrises and sunsets, and then give the pictures to Gracelyn. They make her so happy, she claps her hands."

"A sunset or a sunrise?" asked Lefty. "What do the rest of you think?"

The animals sniffed the air. There was a sharp stinging smell of dust. The sandstorm wasn't far away. They glanced around at each other. They scratched their heads and rubbed their chins, thinking, thinking and thinking some more.

Henry Hawk flapped a wing, "If I may be so bold to comment," he paused for effect. "I have flown very far and very wide and have never been able to get close to a sunrise or a sunset. I don't think we could get close enough to package one up."

Dot twitched her nose. "There might already be a sunset and a sunrise at the hospital." I have heard that everyone has a sunset and sunrise every day." The animals nodded in agreement. They had heard the same thing.

Lefty smiled at the prairie dog child. "That was a good idea, Little Sally, but let's keep thinking."

The wind swished over the desert in light gusts. It made the yellow Arizona poppies nod to and fro. From Pepper's and Dolly's height, it looked like the flowers were waving to the sky. It was a pretty sight, but the wind was becoming less friendly.

Dolly excitedly pawed the ground with a hoof and shouted for all to hear, "I've got it! I know what we should give Gracelyn. Look!" She pointed a hoof up to the sky. "See? Clouds, there's lots and lots of beautiful clouds. There are puffy ones and wispy ones and curly-cue ones right there in the sky. We can catch some for the gift. Gracelyn will be so happy to have her very own clouds."

"That's right," added Merlin. "When Gracelyn and Terry are up on the sundeck, Terry draws the clouds. Gracelyn tells him the names of the different kinds of clouds."

Little Sally gasped, "*The clouds have names?*" She could hardly believe it.

"Yes," said Dolly, "they're called dunderheads, and pony-tails, and circus clouds."

Pepper nudged Dolly. "Um, dear, that's thunderheads, mares' tails and cirrus clouds."

Dolly tossed her head impatiently. "Cirrus! What kind of a word is cirrus? I think circus clouds sounds much more fun. Let's vote to change their name. I think the clouds would like that," said Dolly with a superior snort.

Pepper sighed, "Oh, for pity's sake," and tossed her head.

"Whatever their names are, they are quite beautiful," agreed Lefty. "What does everyone think of that idea?"

Again, the animals thought and thought and thought. Finally Katie Finch raised a wing tip. "Clouds would be a delightful present for Gracelyn, but how would we get a birthday bow around them?" she asked.

Pixel and Dot each raised a paw, at the same time. "I don't think," said Pixel, "we would have time to catch the clouds . . ."

". . . and wrap them up before they melt away," added Dot.

"They do seem to melt very quickly in the sunlight," said Pixel. "How would we get them to Gracelyn before they disappear?"

Lefty rubbed his chin in thought. "That was a good idea, Dolly, but perhaps the clouds are best seen up in the sky. We want Gracelyn to have something she can enjoy for weeks. Anyone have other ideas?"

The sky was beginning to dim as the sun slipped out of sight. Twilight was upon the animals and still they kept thinking. In a flash, Fiona Flycatcher flapped her wings and pointed to the east. "There, look at that! Isn't it magnificent!" she exclaimed.

The animals looked toward the east. The full moon was rising above the dusty storm clouds on the horizon. It was as orange as the flowers of the jubilee bushes. The moon looked huge above the distant tree tops. It was so beautiful. The animals sighed and watched it in silence. Slowly, the moon slipped higher and higher in the sky, turning from orange to yellow to white. It seemed to shrink as it moved higher in the sky.

Jax turned his head to one side and studied the moon. "How would we pull it down from the sky? Do we have enough string to catch it?" The animals shook their heads.

Since it was getting dark, a few stars began to appear in the east above the storm clouds. Larry Flycatcher thought for a moment. He raised his wing. "What about catching the stars? We could string them together to make a necklace for Gracelyn."

Sunny thought that was a great idea. "I say, my fine-feathered tot, that's a marvelous idea! It would look so lovely on Gracelyn with her long hair."

Jax added, "T'would be a proper necklace. We have enough string for a necklace."

Merlin stood up. "I'm not so sure that would work, even though the necklace would be sparkly and pretty. We've all seen shooting stars, haven't we? Suddenly, there's a bright flash through the sky—*poof*—and the star disappears. What would happen to Gracelyn if one of her stars went shooting off while she was wearing the necklace? It would be quite—*poofy.*"

Sunny looked disappointed. "I hadn't quite sorted that out, dear chap. Good thinking. Still, it was a wonderfully twinkly idea, Larry."

Jerry jumped up and down. "I know! I know! I know! Imagine this! Gracelyn is having a tea party with her friends and the stars go shooting off in *every* direction, *at the same time!* Everyone would dive for cover under the table," he exclaimed breathlessly. "And then all of the . . ."

"Jerry," called his father.

". . . stars would go zap, bang, pop, snap, zoom, zing, pow—all over the room!"

"*Jerry!*"

"It would be like fireworks on the 4th of July!" Jerry Flycatcher blinked up at his dad.

Christopher sighed. "As my son has so excitedly pointed out, it could be quite messy."

The animals continued to discuss the gift. The ideas were good, but no one could think of the perfect gift. Lefty rested his head on a front leg. He tried to remember everything Gracelyn enjoyed. He thought to himself, "Of all the things she loved, what could be the most *birthday-ish*? If I just think hard enough, I'll get an answer."

Lefty remembered when he lived in the plastic-walled house in Gracelyn's room. Terry's drawings decorated the walls. There were pictures of the family, and clouds, and animals, and trees and—something else. Instantly, Lefty knew what the perfect gift was for his dear friend, Gracelyn. He burst out with a shout and waved his friends closer. With great excitement, he told the animals his idea. Their eyes opened wide with delight. Everyone cheered! It was going to be the best birthday gift ever!

Jerry Flycatcher was fluttering up and down so excitedly that his feathers began to pop off. Fiona hugged her son, "Calm down, dear. You won't have any feathers left if you keep that up," she chuckled.

Little Sally had scampered down a prairie dog tunnel and missed hearing the idea. When she popped out, everyone was cheering. "What is it? What is it!? Tell me! Tell me!" she shouted.

Merlin crouched down next to her. "Little Sally, climb on my back and I'll take you to the front." Little Sally yipped with joy and scampered up Merlin's back. She jumped up to the top of his head and held on to his tall ears. She didn't want to fall off. The big dog carefully picked his way among the others as they danced in circles and jumped for joy.

When Lefty told Little Sally about the gift, she shouted with glee. She did a somersault and slid down Merlin's nose. She would have fallen except he caught her with his paw and lowered her to the ground. She giggled up at him, "Thank you, Mr. Merlin! You're the best!" With that, she ran to join her family, skipping and leaping across the sand.

The animals danced and sang "Happy Birthday" just for practice. Pepper and Dolly raced around their corral kicking up their
back legs along with some more dust. They cheered and bucked
until they both began to sneeze. The other animals laughed happily. After all, a sneezing horse can be very funny. Finally, the animals began to calm down. Lefty signaled for the animals to gather
closer.

"Now everyone" explained Lefty, "we must go to our burrows,
beds, and nests. The storm is almost here. We need a good night's
sleep. Let's meet back here when the sun is up. First, we'll decide
who will carry the gift to Gracelyn," he paused for effect. "Then
we'll get to work!"

"Yipppeee!" shouted the animals. A sudden gust of wind
snatched up their cheers and tossed the joyful sound across the
desert. The animals knew the storm was almost upon them. They
quickly told each other good night. Then everyone scampered,
flew, or trotted off to their burrows, nests or beds at Eagle Wings.

4

A Stormy Night

WHILE THE MEETING WAS going on, Gracelyn and Terry were eating dinner in the house. The sun would soon be setting in the west, lighting the desert sky ablaze with color. Radiant shades of gold streamed through bright orange, deep rose, and hot pink clouds. The eastern sky was a hazy, tan color, announcing the approaching dust storm.

After dinner the kids moved to Gracelyn's favorite picture-window that looked out on the courtyard. She spent many hours at the window watching the hummingbirds at the feeders and the flycatchers tending their children. She enjoyed looking at the trellises covered with snail vines which had tightly curled purple petals shaped like little snails. Bees buzzed happily among the flowers, collecting pollen for their honey.

In the center of the courtyard was a fountain surrounded by purple and white-striped petunias, lavender, funnel-shaped desert bluebells, and brilliant white star daisies with yellow centers. The courtyard gate that opened out to the rock garden was framed by rose bushes with red and pink blossoms. The rest of the wall was covered with red hibiscus, Lefty's favorite dessert. Gracelyn pretended that the cascading water in the fountain was singing to her. It was a soft, comforting sound.

Occasionally, a cactus wren, dove, flycatcher, sparrow or finch would come and drink from the fountain. Dad and Mom said that owls and hawks would come at night to drink. Sometimes even the honey bees drank the cool refreshing fountain water. In the spring, Gracelyn often caught sight of a tiny bat or two delicately sipping the water. This evening as Terry and Gracelyn sat by the window, not a single bird, bug, or bat was in sight.

"I wonder where everyone is?" asked Terry. "Even the hummingbirds haven't come to drink from their feeder." He looked around the room for the cats and dogs. "And where are Merlin, Jax, Sunny, Pixel, and Dot? I wonder why they're out so late since they're usually in the house by sunset. They must be up to something."

"They do seem to disappear at the same time, now and then," observed Gracelyn. "What do you suppose they do? If they were kids like us, I'd think they were having secret meetings."

"Wouldn't that be funny," laughed Terry. "Merlin would lead the meeting, Jax and Sunny would take attendance, and Pixel and Dot would make sure everyone sat in nice, straight rows."

Gracelyn giggled. "What would Lefty do?"

"Nip the tail of anyone not paying attention, I'm sure," said Terry. The siblings laughed until a gust of wind hit the house.

"I do hope they get in soon. It's getting windy," Gracelyn said anxiously. Sometimes it scared Gracelyn when a windstorm roared across the desert like an angry sand-spitting dragon. Dust storms came up so suddenly at times. "Terry, can you go up on the deck and look for them?" Terry went out to the courtyard and climbed the steps to the rooftop deck.

Gracelyn waited and thought about the approaching storm. She and her family were safe in the house. She knew her animal friends would be safe because they knew what to do. Dolly and Pepper would turn their tails to the wind and kept their heads down. The rabbits and prairie dogs would stay in their tunnels. The birds would huddle in trees and thick bushes. Lefty would go into his burrow and go to sleep.

The door opened and Terry came back in the house. "You're not going to believe this, Gracie," he said with a grin. "It looks like all the animals are gathered around the corral with Pepper and Dolly. Pixel, Dot, Merlin, Jax and Sunny are out there, too. They're up to something." The siblings exchanged curious looks. They wondered what the animals were doing.

Gracelyn and Terry played a game of chess until it was time for Gracelyn to go to bed. Terry never argued with his parents about Gracelyn's early bedtime because she got tired so easily.

Terry usually waited to do his homework until after his sister went to bed. He didn't want to use any time doing school work when they could be playing games, watching a favorite TV show, or just talking. He wished Gracelyn could stay up as late as he could.

Terry was just about to check on the dogs and cats again when they came trooping in through the pet door, one by one. They looked very pleased with themselves. Pixel and Dot went into Gracelyn's room and leaped onto their cat tree with its rope-covered poles, carpet-covered platforms, cubbyholes, and ramps. Merlin curled up on his bed in a corner of the living room. Jax jumped up on the couch next to Terry. Sunny disappeared into Gracelyn's room. She leaped to the foot of Gracelyn's bed and curled up into a tight little ball.

The wind began to howl louder. They could hear it blowing through the palm trees just outside the front windows. The palm fronds rustled against each other making low swishy tones as if they were whispering to each other.

Terry was sitting on the couch when he heard Mom and Dad turn off the television in the TV room. They soon joined him. "What is it, Terry," asked Mom. "You look worried."

"I am worried, Mom, about Gracie and the operation. Will she be okay?"

Mom glanced at Dad and he nodded. "Let's talk about it," Mom said. "Whenever someone has such an important operation like your sister's, things can go wrong, but not very often. We know that Gracelyn has excellent doctors and nurses. They will do their best and help her to recover. But you need to understand, she has to have this operation or she will be in very serious trouble. She needs this operation to get well."

"Will she be able to sing as much as she wants after the operation?" Terry asked.

"When the doctors fix her heart and she recovers," said Dad, "she should be able to do anything she wants."

"Will we be able to ride Pepper and Dolly together? Maybe even go on trail rides?" asked Terry hopefully. He loved to ride horses, but it was more fun when Gracelyn felt strong enough to go with him.

"We certainly hope so, son," said Dad.

The wind roared louder. It clung to the house, hugging the corners, and grabbing at the tree branches as if trying to slow itself down. Along the two driveways, gravel ghost daisies were buffeted by the wind, nearly pushing them to the ground. They were called gravel ghost daisies because the white flowers grew on tall thin grayish-green stems making the flowers appear to hover above the ground without stems. Terry and Gracelyn liked to watch the flowers dance with the wind after sunset. They would joke about the white flowers being the only "real" ghosts since ghosts and goblins were only make-believe things in their favorite scary stories.

Suddenly, something hit the side of the house and rumbled down the gravel driveway. "Wow," said Terry, "the wind is really strong. That must have been my bucket of baseballs." He glanced toward Gracelyn's room. "I wonder if the noise woke her up. I'll go check."

Terry quietly opened the door and whispered, "Gracie, are you awake?"

Gracelyn sighed. "Yup. What was that loud bang?"

"Just my baseball bucket," said Terry as he slipped in the door and pulled a chair over to her bed. He propped his feet on the bed and leaned back in the chair. "Tomorrow we'll need to pick up trash and plastic junk left behind by the storm. Hopefully I'll find all of my baseballs while we're at it."

"Yeah, and *all of the trash* before any of the animals try to eat it," said Gracelyn eagerly. "It'll make them really sick if they do."

There was a whimper at the door and a soft scratching sound. The door slowly swung open, and Jax and Merlin trotted in. Merlin pushed the door closed with his nose. Jax joined Sunny at the foot of the bed. Pixel and Dot came out of the cubbies in their cat tree and watched from their perch on the top platform. Merlin nosed Terry's hand.

"Why were you guys out so late tonight?" asked Gracelyn sternly.

Merlin lowered his head apologetically. "Woof," he rumbled, trying to sound innocent. "Woof, oof, oof, woof." Merlin walked to another dog bed in the corner and plopped himself down with a grunt.

"Did you hear that?" asked Gracelyn. "I think Merlin just told me a fib." Terry snickered. Merlin snorted and tucked his nose under one paw. Sunny and Jax pretended to have gone straight to sleep. They were curled up like cinnamon rolls. Dot and Pixel started licking their fur, pretending to be too busy to pay attention.

Now that Terry and the animals were with her, Gracelyn felt much safer from the storm, but she was wide awake. "Terry, I've been thinking about my operation."

"Me, too. Are you scared?"

"A little," admitted Gracelyn, "but I want to get better so I can do what other kids can do." The siblings were silent for a while as they listened to the wind. One of the cats yawned, got up, took a few turns, and settled back down.

"Was that Pixel?" asked Gracelyn.

"Naw—had to be Dot," said Terry. "Pixel makes this funny little squeak after he yawns." Terry paused in thought. "Gracie, more than anything, I want this operation for you. I know that your doctors and nurses will do the best they can. I believe that you will get well because God made people smart enough to be doctors and nurses to help all of us be healthy. When your heart is fixed, you'll be able to sing and sing and sing. Everyone loves to hear you sing."

Gracelyn smiled bashfully. "Really?"

"Absolutely," Terry grinned happily. "Look! They agreed." Pixel, Dot, Sunny, Jax, and Merlin had raised their heads and were looking at Gracelyn. "I think they're smiling." Gracelyn laughed and the pets put their heads back down with sighs of contentment.

Suddenly, the wind got much stronger. They heard sand clicking against the windows. A sharp whistle sounded from under the eaves of the house as if a wind elf was playing a flute. The wail of the storm startled everyone in the room. For a few minutes, the sandstorm howled as if it were angry with the house for being in the way. The palm fronds on the palm trees weren't whispering anymore—they were shouting at the storm to go away. Then something metallic, perhaps a soda can, rattled up against the side of the house, paused, then rattled away, bouncing along the gravel driveway. It was a spooky, lonely sound. The can went bounce . . . bounce . . . rattle . . . bounce, as the wind pushed the can to go faster.

"I just thought of something," said Gracelyn. "The storm won't last long. Tomorrow will be another nice day. There are lots more nice days than stormy days. That's what we have to remember when we think about my operation. There will be a few bad days, but then I'll have lots and lots of really good days."

"You're right, Gracie. And I'll stay with you, just like you stayed with me when I fell off the monkey bars and broke my leg. I had to stay in bed, too, and it would have been really boring without you to keep me company. We're not just brother and sister. We're best friends."

"I wish all brothers and sisters could be best friends," said Gracelyn.

Merlin rolled over to his side with a loud, grumbly sigh.

"I think Merlin wants us to be quiet," laughed Terry. "I better go get some sleep, too. Tomorrow is our big game and I don't want to let my team down. The guys are counting on me to hit another homerun like I did in the last game. If you're rested enough, you might be able to watch the whole game."

"Oh, I hope so," said Gracelyn.

"In fact, I have a message for you from all the guys on the team. After you get well, they want you to sing the National Anthem before every big game next school year. It was their idea. Coach liked the idea, too."

Gracelyn beamed. "Really? That would be exciting. And every time you guys hit a home run, I'll be able to jump up and cheer."

Terry held out his fist. They bumped fists and spread their fingers out as they made popping noises. Both children laughed when Merlin rolled to his other side with another disapproving groan, which only made them laugh even more.

"Merlin is telling us to hush," said Gracelyn.

"He's right. I better let you go to sleep," declared Terry. "Have nice dreams."

"You, too," she said as her brother started for the door.

"I have a dream about you sometimes," said Terry. "You know what it is?"

"Tell me," Gracelyn waited eagerly for his answer.

"I dream that someday you will sing and the whole world will listen and be happy."

"You're the best big brother *ever*," she said. "*Ten times over, forever and ever.*"

Terry smiled as he stepped into the hall and closed the door softly.

5

Getting to Work

THE NEXT MORNING, THE animals eagerly gathered at the corral, ready to get started on their plan. Lefty hurried to the front of the group and bobbed his head in greeting.

"I hope everyone slept well despite the sandstorm." They nodded their heads and looked around at each other. Happily, no one was distressed or damaged. "Ok, so we know what we want to give to Gracelyn, but how do we get it to her when she goes to the hospital?"

Before anyone else could answer, Jerry Flycatcher's wing was in the air. "I know! I know! I know!" He could barely contain himself and nearly flopped over. "I vote that we send Mr. and Mrs. Hawk because they can fly to fin-a-tee."

Puzzled, Lizzy and Henry Hawk glanced at each other and then at Jerry. "My dear, what is fin-a-tee?" asked Lizzy.

"You know, fin-a-tee, fin-a-tee. A long way away," answered Jerry. His twin, Larry popped his head up and down, and twirled a wing in circles. He looked a bit like a lop-sided helicopter.

Fiona chuckled at her sons. "Larry, calm down before you land on your head. Jerry, dear, do you mean infinity?"

"Uh-huh! Fin-a-tee, Mommy, that's what I said, fin-a-tee." Jerry puffed out his chest with pride. "I even know how far fin-a-tee is." He grandly placed his wing tips on his hips. "It's one hundred, eighty four miles!"

Larry laughed and smacked his twin on the back with his wing. "No, Jerry, fin-a-tee is *one thousand* eighty *six* miles!"

Henry and Lizzy Hawk smiled at the twins. "My dear boys," drawled Henry, "infinity is much farther than that. It's forever. Not a single animal can fly, run or swim to the end of infinity. That's because there *is* no end." The twins were amazed.

Sunny was confused. She poked a paw at her cousin. "One thousand, eighty six miles? What are miles? I say, dear boy, are they as long as the Eagle Wings fence or as long as the tip of my tail to the tip of my nose?"

Jax thought for a moment. "I believe a mile is once around the Eagle Wings fence."

Henry agreed. "That's about right. You got the idea."

Mrs. Hummingbird spoke up. "Actually, the twins have a point. If once around Eagle Wings is about a mile, how far is the hospital from here? It very well may *seem* like infinity. Who among us can travel great distances?"

"I say, my good lady," spoke up Sunny. "Jax and I have. We came all the way from merry old England. We even crossed the great, big, huge, gigantic, Atlantic Ocean. We should be the ones to carry the gift." The little terrier looked about with her nose high in the air.

Jax muffled a snicker with his paw, tapped his cousin on the shoulder, and whispered, "Listen, Dearie, I dare say, you might be leaving out the most important part of that story. We were on a ship. We weren't exactly dog-paddling across the deep-blue sea, now, were we?"

Sunny sniffed with annoyance. "Well, we did a proper jog about the deck every day. That counts for something." Jax affectionately patted his cousin on the back.

Pepper cleared her throat. "Dolly and I are great runners. Our ancestors ran with the Pony Express. They ran from postal station to postal station carrying mail *and* a rider. Perhaps we should carry the gift." Dolly tossed her head in agreement, as usual. Pepper ruffled her mane and flipped her tail, eager to hear everyone's approval. But the animals were quiet and thoughtful. They were wondering how the horses would get out of their corral.

Lefty considered the matter. "Well, there is another possibility. I remember Gracelyn's mom and dad talking about sending packages by snail mail. I know snails are very slow. Goodness, they're even slower than me. However, Gracelyn's mom mentioned that snail mail is quite reliable. Do any of you want to ask the snails if they would carry the gift?" The animals looked doubtful. No one said anything, however, because they didn't want to hurt the snails' feelings. The poor dears were very, very slow, and leaving behind a slimy trail didn't help matters.

Willie Rabbit raised a paw, "If I may. Rosemary and I can run very fast and hop this way and that. Perhaps we should carry the gift."

Rosemary looked concerned. "What about the children, Willie? Who would want to bunny-sit seventeen children?" Willie had not thought of that.

"I still think Dolly and I should carry the gift," said Pepper, a bit annoyed. "We are the fastest because our legs are the longest. When's the last time you saw any animal other than a horse run in the Kentucky Derby?"

Dot and Pixel looked at each other with confusion. "What is a Kentucky Derby?" whispered Pixel.

Dot meowed, "I thought a Derby was some kind of hat. Do you suppose it's a race where the horses run around wearing hats?"

"They'd have to cut holes in the hats for their ears," Pixel snickered.

Pappy Roadrunner was also annoyed. He flapped his wings and sailed up to the top of a greasewood bush. "I should take the gift! I am a roadrunner. *Road—Runner!* Goodness me, I'm the track coach and will have no problem reaching the hospital. Well, that is if someone can point me in the right direction."

Before anyone could comment, Tommy and Beatrice Prairie Dog scurried to the center of the group. "Perhaps we should take the gift. Not only can we run fast, we can tunnel fast," said Tommy.

Beatrice added, "Just in case we have to go under something, like a freeway, with lots of speeding cars."

Pepper and Dolly snorted. Pappy raced around in a circle. Jax and Sunny scratched their ears. Pixel and Dot licked their paws. Merlin looked at the sky and rolled his bright-blue eyes.

All the animals began expressing their opinions at the same time. No one was doing any listening, except Merlin and Lefty.

Finally, Merlin had an idea. He stood up and barked for silence. Everyone got quiet. "My dear friends, the truth is, all of us have special talents. Any one of us could take the gift to Gracelyn. I could take Gracelyn's gift because my mother taught me how to pull a sled through snow and ice over great distances. But we must think of Gracelyn first. Let's consider Jerry Flycatcher's first suggestion." Merlin looked around at his friends and asked, "What travels the fastest and the straightest to anywhere?"

Once again, Jerry threw his wing into the air. "I know! I know! I know! The wind!" The animals grinned and elbowed each other. They knew the wind was not an animal and could not be asked to do such a thing.

Yet Merlin nodded wisely, "Well spoken, Jerry. You are correct."

The other animals looked confused. Katie Finch asked, "Merlin, how can we ask the wind to carry the gift? We don't speak wind-language."

Merlin smiled patiently. "We don't ask the wind. We *borrow* the wind." And he gestured gallantly toward Henry and Lizzy Hawk. "They have the greatest length of wing. They are the strongest birds at Eagle Wings, and they can fly over great distances. They are our best chance of getting the gift to Gracelyn's hospital. That is, if they are willing to do it."

The animals considered the matter carefully. Pepper stomped a hoof. "I vote," she paused and looked around dramatically. "I vote for—Lizzy and Henry Hawk!"

"Hip-hip-hooray! Hip-hip-hooray!" cheered the animals. But soon they quieted down to hear what the hawks had to say about the proposed task.

The two hawks spoke to each other in hushed tones. Then they huddled with their children. Soft whispers could be heard as each child expressed his or her thoughts on the matter. Lizzy and Henry listened. Then they turned to the group.

Henry announced, "If everyone is in agreement, and our children are cared for while we are gone, then we will carry the gift!"

All the animals erupted with jubilation! Pappy and Nana Roadrunner did a jig right in the middle of everyone. Pepper and Dolly pranced around the corral, swishing their tails in excitement. The prairie dogs clapped their paws with approval. The rabbits hopped about with glee. The birds sang with joy. Pixel and Dot purred with pleasure. Merlin, Sunny and Jax did a three-way high-five as they yipped with delight. Lefty bobbed his head and grinned—as best as turtles can.

Henry put a wing around Lizzy's shoulder. "We are honored and will do our very best."

The bird families promised the hawks that they would watch over their children. Pepper and Dolly volunteered the corral railings as a good hangout for the young hawks. The rabbit and prairie dog children promised to play with the hawk children every day.

"Now we must put the gift together," declared Lefty.

Everyone began running, scampering, flying, walking, or hovering over Eagle Wings. The birds were assigned the job of collecting bits of windblown cloth and snippets of yarn. The dogs, rabbits, and cats collected the essential ingredients. The prairie dogs assembled the gift with Lefty's supervision. The horses pointed out the best places to gather the necessary odds and ends. Using the bits of rag and yarn, the prairie dogs carefully wrapped the gift into four bundles. It took the animals all day, but finally, the gift was completed.

Now the animals watched for signs that Gracelyn and her family were preparing to leave for the hospital. The biggest part of this job fell on the dogs and cats since they lived in the house. One of the five always made sure to be in the house at all times so no clue would be missed.

They didn't have long to wait. Just a few days later, Pixel and Sunny saw Terry set two small suitcases in the living room. They immediately ran out the doggie door to tell Merlin, Jax, and Dot who were lounging in the shade of the ficus tree. The five of them ran back in the house to see what would happen next.

A short time later, Gracelyn's and Terry's grandparents drove up the driveway in their big, blue, four-door truck. Terry saw them from the front window and ran out to greet them with hugs. When Grandpa and Grandma came inside, they hugged Mom and Dad, and of course, Gracelyn.

Grandma told the kids, "Looks like you two are ready to go. We're so glad Gracelyn is going to the hospital in our town. Our house is only a few streets away. We can come see you every day."

"So you two will be coming soon?" Grandpa asked Mom and Dad.

"Yes," answered Mom. "We'll be there in two days. We'll leave right after work. Our neighbors will take care of the animals here at Eagle Wings, and make sure they're fed. Terry, you'll be able to stay with Grandma and Grandpa if Gracelyn needs to rest. If you need to come home at any time, that's okay, too."

Terry shook his head with determination. "I'll be fine, Mom. I want to be with Gracelyn as much as I can."

"We wish we could, too. Dad and I are so sorry we can't be at the hospital the whole time you're there, but we will stay a few days when Gracelyn has her operation. We have some vacation time saved up at work. We will come on weekends as well. But we're going to miss both of you so much!"

The kids hugged their mother. "It's okay, Mom," said Gracelyn. She patted her hand over her heart. "I'll keep you and Dad safe, right here." Everyone hugged each other again.

"We'll call every day to let you know how things are going," reassured Grandpa. "And you can always call us."

After watching the family say their goodbyes, the animals knew it was their turn. Pixel and Dot curled around Gracelyn's legs and purred. She bent down to pet them. They looked up at her and meowed their goodbyes. They walked over to Terry and put their front paws on his knees. He stroked their sleek fur. Merlin, Jax, and Sunny nosed Gracelyn's hand, and then Terry's hand. They wagged their tails together and woofed.

Gracelyn looked up at her parents with shining eyes. "They know how much we'll miss them." The siblings stroked each dog and cat with affection.

Merlin, Sunny, and Jax woofed softly, "Be safe, dear ones."

Pixel and Dot meowed, "We will miss both of you very much."

The final farewells were spoken, hugged, kissed, and nuzzled. Grandpa helped Gracelyn into the truck while Grandma and Terry stowed their suitcases in the back. Mom and Dad watched from the front porch. A few tears trickled down Mom's face and Dad put his arm around her shoulders. Merlin and his pals stepped out on the porch to join them. Slowly, the truck started down the driveway. As they went out the gate, the kids looked back and waved.

Gracelyn's eyes popped wide with surprise. She nudged her brother. "Terry, do you see what I see?"

Terry gasped with disbelief. "It looks like—wow—I think the birds are waving good-bye!" Flycatchers, hawks, roadrunners, doves, cactus wrens, sparrows, finches, owls and hummingbirds were perched on the branches of the trees. Each bird was moving their wings up and down. "And look at the prairie dogs! There's a bunch of 'em popping out of their tunnels!"

Gracelyn grabbed Terry's arm. "Look! Lefty is under the mesquite tree bobbing his head! And look at the rabbits! They're coming from everywhere!"

Terry called out to Grandpa and Grandma, "Look! The animals are waving good-bye!"

Grandpa pressed the brake pedal and put the truck in reverse. Slowly, he backed up so they could see down the driveway. Lefty pushed up on his front legs. The prairie dogs stopped popping around and flicked their tails back and forth. The rabbits sat back on their hind legs and wiggled their noses. Pepper and Dolly were watching from their corral with their heads held high. When they saw Gracelyn and Terry waving, they reared on their back legs and whinnied.

Merlin, Sunny, Jax, Dot, and Pixel sat down and each lifted a front paw in the air. Mom and Dad looked at the five furry friends in amazement. With slack-jawed surprise, Dad and Mom stared at the animals as they waved farewell.

"Wow, even our cats and dogs are waving good-bye!" announced Terry. From the front porch, Sunny, Jax, and Merlin barked, and Pixel and Dot meowed. With that delightful chorus, Dad and Mom laughed and waved to their family.

Finally, the truck began to move down the road. When it had gone completely out of sight, Merlin spun around and dashed off. The others followed and they disappeared around the corner of the house.

"Now, where in the world are they going?" asked Mom as she shook her head in bewilderment.

In no time, the animals at Eagle Wings were gathered at the horse corral. The prairie dogs retrieved the four secret bundles from among the hay bales. Henry and Lizzy Hawk swooped in and landed on the top of the bales. The prairie dogs securely fastened a bundle to each leg of the hawks.

"Not too heavy I trust?" asked Tommy Prairie Dog. The hawks shook their heads and lifted each foot to show that the bundles would be no problem as they flew. The animals cheered and waved as the hawks flexed their powerful wings and soared into the air.

"Tally-ho, and off you go!" shouted Jax and Sunny in unison as they danced a jig.

Merlin observed, "They will have no problem following the truck, especially with their sharp eyes." Everyone watched Lizzy and Henry climb higher in the sky.

The two birds circled once, calling good-bye to their children. The hawk children waved. "We promise to be good," they called. "Be safe and come back soon!"

Lizzy and Henry spotted the bright-blue truck. Their powerful wings stroked the air. The animals cheered as they watched the hawks fly out of sight.

6

The Gift is Delivered

EVERYONE GATHERED AROUND THE young hawks. The little birds had been excited about the gift, but now they missed their mom and dad. Several of the youngest children began to cry.

"We already want our Mommy and Daddy to come back," they peeped.

"I know it's hard and a little scary," Merlin said gently to the unhappy hawk children. "Each of you will need to be as brave as your parents. But you're not alone." The big husky gestured toward the animals. "Look at everyone around you. We will help you wait for your parents to return. We can think up games to play and adventure stories to tell. It'll help the time go by quickly, you'll see." Reassured, the little hawks looked around at their friends and smiled.

Little Sally Prairie Dog scampered over to the young birds. "Let's play tag" she said, tapping one of them on the wing, "You're it!" The children began to dart about and more children joined in. It was fun and cheered everyone up. The other animals returned to their daily routines. They were prepared for the long wait until Gracelyn and Terry returned home. They would be waiting just as eagerly for Henry and Lizzy Hawk to return.

The determined red-tailed hawks flew high and fast, and they never lost sight of the bright-blue truck. The hawks found food and roosted in a tree next to the hotel when the family stopped for the night. Henry and Lizzy missed their children and friends at Eagle Wings. They were tired, but happy when they arrived at Gracelyn's hospital the next day. They retreated to a nearby tree to rest. Lizzy and Henry could see Gracelyn and Terry through the glass wall of the hospital room.

The next day, Mom and Dad came to the hospital. The nurses came for Gracelyn and Terry, Mom, and Dad left with them. Hours later, the nurses brought Gracelyn back. Grandma and Grandpa were there with Terry, Mom, and Dad. Gracelyn was awake and talking. She was sleepy, but very happy to see her family. Mom and Dad told the kids that they would go with Grandma and Grandpa to their house, and be back in a few hours. They knew Gracelyn needed to rest, but she asked if Terry could stay.

Henry and Lizzy knew it was their turn. They landed on the little wall outside the patio door. They began to sing in their best hawk-melody. "Happy Birthday to you. Happy Birthday to you. Happy Birthday, dear Gracelyn. *Happy Birthday to you!*"

Terry and Gracelyn looked out the glass wall when they heard the birds' shrill song. The kids recognized the two birds. Gracelyn clapped her hands with delight.

"Terry, those are the red-tailed hawks from Eagle Wings! That's Henry and Lizzy!" Gracelyn exclaimed with surprise. "They had to fly for two days to get here!"

Terry shook his head in bewilderment. "I guess they did, but why? Oh look, there's something tied to their legs. I'll go see what it is." He opened the sliding-glass door. The birds tilted their heads from side to side. Then each held one leg out, then the other. Terry understood what they wanted. "Just hold still Lizzy. You too, Henry. There you go. Okay. I got 'em."

He hurried back into the room and showed the bundles to Gracelyn. Carefully, she untied the bit of yarn around the first cloth bundle. It looked like the yarn and cloth the kids scattered for the birds at nest building time. Terry watched as his sister unfolded the scraps of cloth. Fold by fold, the secret inside was revealed. Grace-lyn's eyes popped wide open. Both children gasped with surprise. There, inside, nestled at the center of each cloth, were—*seeds.*

There were dozens of seeds in each of the four bundles. There were all kinds of seeds. There were flat ones, round ones, oval ones, tiny ones and not so tiny ones. There were tan seeds, brown seeds, and black seeds. There were rough seeds and smooth seeds.

Gracelyn's eyes were shining with joy as she looked out at Henry and Lizzy. "This is for my birthday, isn't it?" she asked. "How did you know it was my birthday?"

"Lefty told us." They chirped with their usual *keeer-r-r, keeer-r-r.* "He heard your mom and dad talking about it. All of us at Eagle Wings wanted you to have a birthday gift while you were away. We planned and worked together to give you this gift."

Gracelyn and Terry laughed. "I don't know what they said," exclaimed Terry, "but it sounded like they answered you!"

"Terry, quick, give them some water in that cup and take this old blanket out there. They can make it into a nest on the patio and sleep there until they're ready to fly home. Isn't this exciting? I can't wait to tell Mom and Dad. And I *really* can't wait to see what kind of plants all these seeds will make." Terry filled the cup with water and placed it next to the blanket on the patio. This way the children could keep watch over the birds while they rested.

The hawks fluttered to the patio and drank the water. It was cool and refreshing. They pulled and tugged at the old blanket until they had made a comfortable nest. Soon, they were settled in for a much deserved rest.

Terry collected the seeds from the four pieces of cloth. Gracelyn, Lizzy, and Henry watched while Terry planted the seeds in the unused flowerbeds.

"Be sure to water them really good," urged Gracelyn after Terry patted the soil firmly over the last seed. The hawks squawked *keeer-r-r* with approval. They were pleased that Terry did such a good job.

Terry used the water pitcher from his sister's bedside table and generously watered each seed. He pulled a chair up to the glass wall and sketched the two hawks as they rested. He used his colored pencils to show off the beautiful design of the birds' feathers. When he held the picture for Gracelyn to see, she smiled with admiration.

It was hard for the children to go to sleep that night. They kept looking out the sliding-glass door to check on their friends. Henry and Lizzy never twitched, squirmed or wiggled. They slept through the night with their heads tucked under a wing, huddled close together. Finally, Gracelyn fell asleep, too. Terry checked on the hawks one last time and settled down on his cot next to his sister's bed.

The red-tailed hawks woke early the next morning. They tapped on the glass with their beaks. Gracelyn waved and blew kisses when she saw the hawks spread their wings to prepare to leave. Henry and Lizzy flapped their strong wings and flew to the top of the wall. They turned and waved a wing tip at their young friends. Terry quickly drew a sketch of the hawks as they were about to spring into flight. Up, up, up, they flew until they were out of sight.

Their mission was a success. Lizzy and Henry were on their way back to Eagle Wings. They were eager to get home and wished they could fly night and day. The hawks couldn't wait to see their children. They were also eager to tell their friends that Gracelyn's operation was over, she was recovering, and the gift was delivered. It was a welcome sight to the hawks when they finally spied Eagle Wings.

The animals took turns keeping watch for their return. It was Tommy Prairie Dog's turn to be on the lookout when Henry and Lizzy swooped in and landed on the railing of the horse corral. Tommy Prairie Dog, Pepper, and Dolly jumped with joy.

"Hey, everybody! They're here! They're here!" shouted the happy friends.

The clever prairie dog snatched up a stick and started beating it against the water tank in the corral. The horses whinnied, and kicked up their heels, stirring up clouds of dust. Everyone rushed over to the corral as fast as they could. The animals, especially their children, cheered to see that Mr. and Mrs. Hawk were safely home. The hawk family excitedly greeted each other with hugs of joy. Lizzy and Henry described how both Gracelyn and Terry were thrilled with Gracelyn's birthday gift and how carefully Terry had planted and watered the seeds. They didn't leave out a single detail. The animals were also excited because they knew that Gracelyn and Terry would be home soon.

Back at the hospital, the sun shone down on the patio ground. The seeds felt the warmth of the sun and the moisture of the water. The children saw that fragile green seedlings were beginning to lift out of the dark earth. Their leaves reached up for the light. Their roots drank in the water Terry gave them every day. The young plants grew and grew and grew.

More days went by until one morning Terry pulled the curtain back so Gracelyn could see their little garden. He cried out with delight, "Gracie, look!"

"Oh, wow!" Gracelyn cried, clapping her hands with joy. The plants had blossomed. Flowers filled the little garden. There were violet desert verbena, pink Apache plume, red fairy dusters, yellow and orange Arizona poppies, white desert lilies, and lavender desert bluebells. There were even purple and white petunias just like the flowers Mom and Grandma had planted in the courtyard by Gracelyn's favorite window. There were golden desert snapdragons, white monkey flowers, red Indian paintbrushes, white daisy desert stars, and blue sapphire wooly stars.

"What an amazing and wonderful gift!" Gracelyn exclaimed. "They made sure I had a little bit of home with me here at the hospital. Seeing all these flowers with such pretty colors and shapes makes me so happy."

Weeks passed and the flowers grew even more. Gracelyn had recovered from the operation and was now working with her doctors and nurses to build her strength. She often became tired and sometimes didn't want to do the exercises. At times, she even became discouraged and wanted, very badly, to go home. Then the colorful flowers reminded Gracelyn that she was dearly loved by the animals at Eagle Wings. They had given her a gift from their hearts. Each day that another plant blossomed, Gracelyn knew she was another day closer to going home. Dad and Mom called every day and came to visit on the weekends. Grandpa and Grandma visited at the hospital every day. Gracelyn was never lonely. Even when Terry left to get something to eat, she could enjoy her flowers. Sometimes a gentle breeze would stir the delicate petals as if they were waving to her. Gracelyn would smile and feel so much better.

Gracelyn wanted to thank the animals for her gift in a very special way. She thought of an idea and shared it with Terry. He agreed that it was a great idea. The kids got to work. Terry drew each type of flower on a separate sheet of paper, and Gracelyn colored them with crayons. Staying busy made the days pass quickly. The last day at the hospital finally arrived.

"Have you thought about your birthday party, Gracie?" asked Terry.

"I sure have," exclaimed Gracelyn. "The party will be so much fun since everyone will be there. I'll be really glad to be home, too. I miss having Jax and Sunny keep my feet warm in bed. I like to hear Merlin make those woofy noises in his sleep. Isn't it funny when dogs do that? And I can't wait to see Dot and Pixel leaping up and down their cat trees. They look like they're flying." She wrinkled her nose and giggled. She thought for a moment. "I've missed watching our birds drink from the fountain and the feeders. Dolly and Pepper must be wondering why we haven't brought them carrots. We haven't given hibiscus blossoms to Lefty. And the rabbits and prairie dogs must be missing our leftover lettuce and greens. I know Dad and Mom are taking good care of them, but I hope the animals aren't worried because they haven't seen us for so long."

Terry thought for a moment. "I'm sure they're okay. I bet Lefty told them why we have been gone," he said with a wink. The kids looked at each other and laughed. They knew it was silly to think that their desert tortoise understood things like operations and hospitals.

With their suitcases packed and ready to go, the children waited eagerly for Grandma and Grandpa to come get them. They looked forward to getting home so their family and animal friends at Eagle Wings would be together once again. And then, they would have a great, big, fun, exciting, birthday party with games and music and lots of yummy food—for Gracelyn!

7

Time for the Party

It was a joyous day when Grandpa drove the big, blue truck through the gate and down the driveway. Everyone came out of the house to welcome them home. There were hugs and smiles and more hugs. Merlin was yipping and yodeling with glee. Siberian Huskies yodel when they get *really* excited. The children laughed to hear the big, brawny dog making such funny noises. Pixel and Dot took turns rubbing against the ankles of Gracelyn and Terry. Jax and Sunny behaved as if they were ping pong balls and bounced all over the place. Pepper and Dolly were bucking and whinnying with joy. Prairie dogs popped in and out of their burrows. Rabbits jumped over each other, under each other, and over each other again! They looked like they were hopping in two directions at once. The hawks, roadrunners, wrens, owls, sparrows, finches, flycatchers, hummingbirds, and doves soared and swayed. They swooped and swung. Birdsong filled the air.

Gracelyn let out a gasp when everyone went into the house. There was a sign across the top of her favorite window in huge, brightly colored letters. *Welcome Home Gracelyn! Happy Birthday!* There was a big, dark-chocolate candy bar with a bow on it propped against the window. The fact that her birthday had been weeks before didn't matter of course. The birthday sign made her feel happy, as well as the dark-chocolate candy bar since it was her favorite. She slipped the candy bar into her pocket when Mom gave her an encouraging nod.

The family gathered in the living room to talk about everything that had happened since the children left for the hospital. Terry and Gracelyn described the wonderful birthday gift brought by Henry and Lizzy. Dad and Mom, and their grandparents were surprised and thrilled at what the children told them.

Gracelyn and Terry hurried from the house to visit Pepper, Dolly, Lefty, and all their animal friends. The dogs and cats went with them. Merlin touched noses with Lefty and barked a happy greeting to his friend. Gracelyn plucked some hibiscus flowers from a bush and gave them to the desert tortoise.

"Here you go, Lefty," said Gracelyn. "I'm sorry you've had to wait so long for dessert." Lefty smiled, as best as turtles can, of course, and munched the blossoms contentedly.

The kids ran to the corral with carrots for the horses. Dolly and Pepper nickered happily and rushed over to the railing. They were so glad to see Gracelyn and Terry, they almost forgot about the carrots.

"Thank you," neighed Pepper and Dolly when the children waved the carrots under the horses' noses. Gracelyn and Terry laughed to see the horses toss their heads with joy as they ate their treats.

"It sure is good to be home," said Gracelyn. "I'm so glad you stayed with me in the hospital, Terry. I would have been really lonesome without you."

"I'm glad to be home, too," said Terry, "but I would have been bored around here while you were in the hospital. It's no fun hitting baseballs by myself, and no one else will play chess or card games with me. I would have been lonesome, too."

Gracelyn knew that Terry could have invited any of his friends over. She smiled at him as she pulled her chocolate bar from her pocket. She tore off the wrapper, broke the candy in two, and gave half to Terry. They smiled at each other as they bit into the semi-sweet candy.

Dot and Pixel curled around Gracelyn's and Terry's ankles and purred. Sunny and Jax skipped around and occasionally jumped on their legs until they ruffled the scrappy little dogs' ears. Merlin pressed his nose against their hands until they scratched his head. The animals were very happy to have their human friends back home with them.

That night, Pixel, Dot, Merlin, Sunny, and Jax trotted off to Gracelyn's bedroom. They huddled together, softly woofing and meowing as they discussed the party. They settled down for the night after they finally agreed on a plan.

The next morning, the sun looked like it was encased in frosted glass as it shimmered behind high, ice-crystal clouds. The day was cooler than usual for this time of year. The children woke up refreshed after their first night back home. They got dressed and were surprised to see breakfast was already on the table. Everyone ate quickly and cleared the table. There was a lot to do to get ready for the party. Everyone got to work preparing food and setting up tables and chairs. It wasn't long before neighbors and more family showed up. They all pitched in to help with the party preparations.

The animals also began their preparations. The first and hardest part of their plan involved Merlin. He had to open two gates for the horses, first the garden gate, and then the corral gate. No one noticed when Merlin slipped out the dog-door. He waited in the courtyard until Mom went out to take Lefty some lettuce in the rock garden. She left the courtyard gate open so Merlin was able to go into the rock garden to open the garden gate. Being a clever dog, Merlin rose up on his hind legs and grasped the gate handle with his teeth. He pulled down. The gate swung open, and he trotted out to the horses' corral.

"Ah good!" nickered Pepper, "you made it."

"Of course I did, old friend," woofed Merlin with a twinkle in his eye. "The gate was no problem." He was rather pleased with himself. He didn't mention that he had practiced opening it while the children were at the hospital.

However, the corral gate was different from the rock garden gate. This one might be a problem. Merlin trotted around to the corral gate and again, rose up on his hind legs. With his nose, he lifted the latch. Before he could move again, the latch fell back into place. Merlin took a deep breath and tried again. Ever so carefully, the patient dog, again, lifted the latch with his nose. Then quickly, before it could fall back into place, he pushed the latch bolt over with his muzzle. The gate creaked open a few inches. The horses snorted with delight and Merlin woofed with satisfaction.

"Thanks," whinnied Dolly. Too excited to stand still, they trotted around the corral kicking up their feet just for good measure. Even though the gate was open, they needed to stay in the corral for now. It wasn't time yet.

"Thanks, Merlin," snorted Pepper as she tossed her head.

"No problem!" barked the big dog, and he trotted back to the rock garden. He slipped in through the gate, leaving it open a few inches.

Lefty was waiting for Merlin in the rock garden. "Mission accomplished?" asked Lefty.

"Yes! Everything's ready," woofed Merlin.

"Most excellent!" Lefty bobbed his head with excitement.

Soon cars and trucks began to arrive with more party guests. They came in the house carrying dishes of food and brightly wrapped presents. Several people volunteered to help in the kitchen and carry food to the picnic tables set up in the rock garden. Out at the gazebo, Grandpa lit the charcoal in the barbeque so he and Dad could grill the hot dogs and hamburgers. Mom pulled her freshly baked hamburger and hot dog buns from the oven. Some of the neighbors helped set up a few last-minute decorations out in the garden while Terry placed party favors along the tables. Several of the neighborhood kids inflated colored balloons with a helium tank then tied the balloons to rocks placed down the centers of all the tables. Since the curvy driveway was lined with rocks, Terry and his friends didn't have far to go to find suitable ones for table decorations.

Terry and Gracelyn had not forgotten the special way they were going to thank their animal friends for the birthday gift. Terry took each drawing of the different flowers from his sketch book. At the top of each picture, the kids wrote *Thank You*. Then they made a list with the names of every four-legged or winged friend at Eagle Wings. Gracelyn wrote this message under the names: *Dearest Friends, the birthday gift of flowers, full of life and color, made me so happy! You brought a part of "home" to me while I was away. I will never forget your loving gift! Your friend, Gracelyn*

They took the flower pictures out to the picnic tables and fastened them to the strings tied to the balloons. A gentle wind made the brightly-colored balloons sway and turn so everyone could see the thank-you-notes. They taped the list of names to the trunk of the huge ficus tree so that their friends and family would know about the gift.

"Look, Terry," said Gracelyn, "the breeze is helping the balloons get everyone's attention. I hope all the animals will see the pictures. I'm going to put them in a scrapbook along with photographs and stories about this very special birthday party."

Back in the house, Grandma put a few finishing touches on the condiment trays before volunteers carried them out to the picnic tables. She picked up a bowl of potato salad and started to carry it outdoors when she spied the terriers sitting on the couch. Both Jax and Sunny sat very quietly as they watched everyone walking in and out of the house.

"Is there something wrong with Sunny and Jax?" Grandma asked Mom who had just come back in to get more cups. "I swear those little scallywags look like they're up to something."

A few friends helping out in the kitchen looked around at the dogs and laughed. A neighbor commented, "Yeah, they *are* acting unusually un-bouncy, especially for those two."

Jax and Sunny glanced at each other, jumped down from the couch, and trotted out of the dog-door. In the rock garden, they joined Merlin who was lying under the ficus tree.

Jax woofed, "Apparently, our secret is hard to keep, even if we *don't say a word!* Perhaps we should chase each other around the tree, just to appear normal?" Sunny and Merlin woofed a few snickers.

The three dogs went back in the house to find the cats. Pixel and Dot were lying on a window ledge watching out the front picture window.

"We think everyone is here now," purred Dot. It was the cats' job to keep an eye out for all the party guests.

"I'll go tell the others," woofed Merlin. "Jax, Sunny, come help." The three friends went out the dog-door to the rock garden.

Outside, under the shade of the big ficus tree, everyone was talking and sipping lemonade and iced tea. Pixel and Dot popped out of the dog-door and ran to Merlin, Jax and Sunny.

"Mom's bringing the cake out! Is everyone ready?" meowed Dot breathlessly. Merlin looked around and saw that the animals at Eagle Wings were ready.

Mom came out carrying a huge cake decorated with white frosting and pink roses. Gracelyn turned around and saw the big, beautiful cake for the first time.

"*Happy Birthday, Gracelyn!*" they all shouted together.

Gracelyn clapped her hands with delight. Everything looked so pretty and festive. "Oh thank you, everyone! It looks wonderful! This is the best birthday party I've ever had."

Her friends and family clapped and cheered. Dad and Grandpa got busy cooking the hot dogs and hamburgers. Bowls of potato salad, garden salad, and chips were passed around.

Dad called out, "Come and get it! Food's ready! Food's hot! Let's eat!" Everyone cheered. Gracelyn was sent to the front of the line and she got a hot dog and a burger. She didn't want to miss out on anything. The party-goers talked, laughed and filled their plates. But Gracelyn didn't start eating until she found Lefty sitting near his burrow. She plucked off a few hibiscus blossoms and gave them to him.

"There you go, Lefty," she said as she placed the flowers in front of him. Lefty bobbed his head to say thank you. Gracelyn ran into the house and put the dogs' and cats' food bowls on a tray. She filled each of them with food. She hurried outside and set a bowl in front of Merlin, then Pixel, then Sunny, then Dot, and then Jax. They woofed and meowed their thanks before they happily gobbled down their food.

Everyone ate, and talked, and laughed, and ate some more. A cool wisp of wind floated through the rock garden. The sun was hiding behind puffy clouds, keeping the day cool. Finally, it was time to cut the birthday cake. Grandma lit the twelve pink candles. Gracelyn squeezed her eyes shut, made her wish, and blew the candles out. Everyone clapped. The cake was cut and generous slices were handed out. Then something odd happened.

Gracelyn was the first to notice. Merlin, Dot, Sunny, Jax, and Pixel stood up together and walked over to Gracelyn. In a perfect line, they faced her and sat down in a row at her feet. Several others noticed the pets and commented to the people sitting around them. The partygoers started looking around. The birds at Eagle Wings had drifted in, several at a time, and perched on the lowest branches of the trees. There were flycatchers, roadrunners, hummingbirds, sparrows, cactus wrens, finches, hawks, burrowing owls, and even doves.

Terry called over to where their mother sat with Grandma and Grandpa. "Mom," he asked excitedly, "do you see this?" He pointed to the birds in the trees. Mom looked around and nudged Grandma. She looked around and nudged Grandpa, who sat his fork down and stared. Everyone had noticed.

One of the neighbor children pointed a finger at the walls of the rock garden and shouted, "Look!" One by one, the entire prairie dog clan slipped in through the gate and climbed up the wall. They moved in single file across the top of the walls until everyone had room. Then they faced Gracelyn and sat down.

Someone else pointed toward the gate. The rabbit families, including cousins, aunts and uncles, were hopping in to the rock garden. They assembled behind Merlin and the others, faced Gracelyn, and sat down. Then a hush fell on every child and every adult. No one dared to make a sound. Softly at first, then louder, a clop, clop, clop was heard. The rock garden gate swung wide open. Pepper and Dolly stepped through the gate to join the gathering. Everyone let out a gasp at the sight of the proud horses, their heads held high. They tossed their heads once in Gracelyn's direction and stood still. Lefty came around in front of Merlin and faced Gracelyn.

Then the most amazing thing happened! Merlin stood up. Quietly, each and every animal came to attention. Then, together, every creature extended a front leg, lowered his or her head and bowed to their friend, Gracelyn. The children and adults caught their breath. They stared wide-eyed at the birds, the rabbits, the prairie dogs, the horses, the cats, the dogs, and the tortoise.

Terry went to Mom and whispered in her ear. She smiled and hurried into the house. When she came out, she was carrying her violin. Terry pulled a chair over to Gracelyn and whispered in her ear. She whispered to Mom. They both smiled and nodded and Gracelyn stood up. She looked around at her family, her friends, her neighbors, and all the animals at Eagle Wings. Everyone waited with bated breath, eager to see what would happen next.

Gracelyn put her hand to her heart and bowed her head in thankfulness. Then she lifted her head, took a wonderful, deep breath, and began to sing in a strong, clear voice. Mom joined in with her violin. The most beautiful, sweet sound lilted through the air.

> *Amazing Grace, how sweet the song,*
> *That saved a child like me.*
> *I once was lost, but not for long.*
> *Was bound but now I'm free.*

Her angelic voice drifted from ear to ear and heart to heart. A gentle puff of air touched the trees and their leaves swayed in time with Gracelyn's song. Then the animals joined in, humming and softly stamping their feet in harmony.

> *It's Grace that sought my fearful heart.*
> *And Grace, my fears relieved.*
> *How swiftly did that Grace impart,*
> *True hope, when first believed.*

The walls of the rock garden echoed the melodious notes. Then the birds joined in. Their song blended with Gracelyn's voice and Mom's violin. The rock garden came alive with marvelous music.

> *Through many illnesses this far,*
> *I have already passed.*
> *I need not wish upon a star,*
> *Since Grace will always last.*

Standing next to his sister, Terry began to sing, too, and Dad joined them. Then everyone began to sing.

> *You all have shown love to me.*
> *Your trust will be my cure.*
> *Grace will my salvation be,*
> *As long as I endure.*

The harmony of the animals humming merged with the melody of human voices. Gracelyn's delicate soprano voice rose with the trill of the songbirds. Mom's violin blended beautifully with the voices of Eagle Wings.

Amazing Grace, how sweet the song,
That saved a child like me.
I once was lost, but not for long,
Was bound, but now I'm—FREE!

Gracelyn threw her arms around her brother. Mom and Dad joined in the hug. Grandma and Grandpa encircled the four of them. Gracelyn laughed, *"This is the best group hug—ever!"*

The neighbors and friends laughed with happiness, clapped and cheered. No one wanted the beautiful song to stop. They wished the music would go on forever, *and it did*—in each person's memory. From that day on, the magic of that moment was forever sealed in every heart, every mind, and every soul. This day of blessing would last in fond remembrance. It would never, ever, be forgotten, *ten times over, forever and ever!*